SOLD

THE SECRET VALLEY

By the same author

The Hiding-Place

The Mail-Coach Driver

The Night of the Storm

The Post Rider

The Stone People

THE SECRET VALLEY

by

ELIZABETH RENIER

Illustrated by Gavin Rowe

HAMISH HAMILTON
LONDON

For Andrew with love

HAMISH HAMILTON CHILDREN'S BOOKS

Published by the Penguin Group
27 Wrights Lane, London W8 5TZ, England
Viking Penguin Inc., 40 West 23rd Street, New York, New York 10010, U.S.A.
Penguin Books Australia Ltd, Ringwood, Victoria, Australia
Penguin Books Canada Ltd, 2801 John Street, Markham, Ontario, Canada L3R 1B4
Penguin Books (N.Z.) Ltd, 182–190 Wairau Road, Auckland 10, New Zealand

Penguin Books Ltd, Registered Offices: Harmondsworth, Middlesex, England

First published in Great Britain 1988 by
Hamish Hamilton Children's Books

British Library Cataloguing in Publication Data
Renier, Elizabeth
The secret valley.—(Antelope).
I. Title II. Rowe, Gavin
823'.914[J] PZ7

ISBN 0-241-12257-0

Filmset in Baskerville by
Katerprint Typesetting Services, Oxford
Printed in Great Britain at the
University Press, Cambridge

Chapter I

"WHAT SHALL WE do this morning?" asked Jessica.

"Go exploring," answered James, her ten-year-old twin. "A long way from the house so we don't hear Mama grumbling."

Cook, who was making a suet pudding, slapped his hand as he tried to grab some raisins.

"You must make allowances for your mother," she said. "She didn't want to leave Bath to live in the country."

"But it's so much more interesting

here in Devonshire," Jessica said. "And Papa likes it."

"Your father has his work. Besides, your mother is town-bred and brought up to lead a lady's life, not that of a country doctor's wife. It will take her a little while to get used to it."

"I hope it will be only a *little* while," said James. "She's always so cross and never laughs like she used to."

"She misses her friends. Now, be off, the pair of you and let me get on."

"And take a basin with you," added

Molly, the cheerful maid-of-all-work at Foxton House. "There are plenty of blackberries along the hedge by Badgers' Wood."

The September sun was warm as the twins set off along the lane. Bees and

butterflies were gathering nectar from the wild flowers. Goldfinches and linnets twittered joyously as they fed on thistle seeds. At Deerleap Farm the twins stopped to watch the harvesters loading wagons with corn to be carted away and stacked in the great Dutch barn. Then, as they walked on towards the forge, they saw Squire Basset, impatiently waiting for his big, grey horse to be shod.

The Squire was a huge man with a loud voice and a quick temper. He owned most of the farms and cottages in the district, which meant that almost everyone depended on him for their livelihood. The men touched their hats to him, the women and children bobbed curtsies. The twins had wondered if they should do the same but their mother had said, "Certainly not. *We* are not beholden to him in any way. You will show him politeness but not servility."

So now, when the Squire demanded, "Where are you two going?" James answered firmly, "Just for a walk."

"What's that basin for?"

"We're going to pick blackberries," answered Jessica.

"Don't you trespass in my woods," the Squire shouted.

"I didn't think blackberries grew in woods," said James, a little too pertly.

The Squire strode over to them, rapping his whip against his riding-boot. "Are you being cheeky?" he demanded.

With the big man looming over him, James was tempted to touch his cap like the local boys but he faced up to the Squire and said politely, "No, sir. I was just making sure we don't go where we're not allowed."

"You'll learn soon enough if you do. Either my gamekeeper will catch you or you'll have a leg broken in a trap. So stay away from anywhere marked PRIVATE. Understand?"

"Yes, sir," answered the twins in unison.

"What a horrid man!" exclaimed Jessica when they were out of earshot. "I wish *he'd* get his leg caught in a trap."

The gate at the entrance to the field

alongside Badgers' Wood did not have a PRIVATE notice on it and they were sure Molly would not have sent them there if it was forbidden. Jessica was happy gathering the juicy berries, the sun warm on her back, but James soon tired of it and wandered off.

Presently he called, "Come and look, Jess."

She ran to join him. "What have you found?"

"A deep valley, sort of hidden away. There's not a farm or cottage in sight. Let's climb down and explore."

"It looks a bit creepy," said Jessica.

"That's what makes it exciting! Come on."

Jessica left the basin of blackberries beside the hedge and followed James down the steeply sloping field. The ground was rough, with tufts of coarse grass, and Jessica was glad she had put on her button boots. Soon they were pushing their way through tall golden bracken. It was very hot in the enclosed valley but at last they came to a grassy bank beside a stream, which tinkled and gurgled between moss-covered boulders and disappeared into a copse.

"It's not creepy here," exclaimed Jessica. "This is a lovely place." She knelt to trail her fingers in the water.

"Let's explore the copse," suggested James, but Jessica was happy beside the stream.

Even after James had disappeared amongst the trees, Jessica did not mind being alone. It was very quiet, but it was a friendly sort of quiet, with the water chattering companionably and a buzzard mewing, far overhead. Jessica lay down on the short grass and happily watched the soaring bird and was not pleased when James, approaching silently, hissed in her ear, "Come with me. I've found something exciting!"

Jessica was reluctant to move but James pulled her to her feet and hurried her along the bank and into the copse.

They followed a narrow track which James said had been made by deer or badger and where low branches caught at Jessica's clothes and knocked her hat off. Where the trees thinned, James stopped and pointed.

Half-hidden by bushes and tall grasses was a collection of dilapidated buildings, with tumbledown walls and sagging roofs of thatch. The little gardens were overgrown and nettles thrived in the small enclosures where once the family pig had been kept.

"What do you think happened?" asked Jessica, feeling she had to whisper. "Lots of people must have lived here. Why don't they any more?"

"Perhaps there was a fire," James suggested. "Although nothing looks burned. Perhaps they were all killed off by the Black Death."

"What's that?"

"The plague. Thousands of people died. It was a long time ago."

Jessica shuddered. "I don't like this place. Let's go back now."

"Not yet. I want to have a look round. There might be . . . "

He broke off as Jessica clutched his arm.

"Look," she whispered. "There's smoke coming from amongst the trees further on."

"Then *someone* must live here still," whispered James excitedly. "Let's go and see. But be quiet."

Jessica did not want to go with him but neither did she want to be left alone in this forlorn and silent place, so different from the friendly quiet beside the sunlit stream. Reluctantly she crept along behind him, telling herself that the feeling of being watched was just imagination, yet glancing over her shoulder to make sure.

Suddenly she remembered how Molly had replied, when James asked if there were ghosts at Foxton House.

"Not here. But there *are* places nearby where folks won't venture because of ghosties. Hidden-away places where weird moaning sounds have been heard."

This was surely such a place, thought Jessica, and tugged at James' coat.

"Let's go back. I'm frightened."

"Don't be stupid! There's nothing to be frightened of. Unless . . . "

"Unless what?" she asked fearfully.

"The smoke could be coming from a poacher's hide-out," said James with relish. "Or even smugglers'."

That made Jessica even more nervous.

They were creeping between the derelict buildings when James stopped so abruptly that Jessica cannoned into him. As she cried out, James whispered crossly, "Be quiet! I can hear someone moving about. If they *are* poachers or smugglers they won't want to be discovered."

Jessica peered over his shoulder, her heart thumping uncomfortably. A wisp of smoke rose from the ivy-covered chimney of a one-storey cottage set back a little from the stream. An attempt had been made to repair the walls and prop up the sagging thatch. From the branch of a twisted tree beside the rickety door hung a dead rabbit.

James gripped his sister's wrist and whispered into her ear. "Someone's amongst the trees above the cottage. We'd better crouch down behind this wall."

Peering through gaps in the stonework they saw a man come out from the trees, carrying a bundle of firewood. He was poorly dressed, his trousers and coat threadbare and patched, his boots laced with string and gaping at the toes. A felt hat hid his face but he walked with a stoop like an old man, and he stumbled on the doorstep as he entered the cottage.

"*He* doesn't look like a smuggler," whispered Jessica with relief. "And look, over there by the stream."

Kneeling on the bank was an old woman, filling a pail with water. Her clothes were as threadbare as the man's and she wore a grey shawl over straggly white hair. As she rose stiffly and started towards the cottage the man reappeared and called, "Wait, Martha, let me help you."

He was taking the pail from her when a grass tickled James' nose and he sneezed loudly. The old couple dropped the pail and, clinging together, stared towards the wall. They looked so frightened that the twins showed themselves.

"I'm sorry I scared you," said James, but the couple still looked terrified.

As the twins approached them, they

backed away, holding tightly to each other.

The man said, in a quavery voice, "You'm come to take us. But we'll not go."

"We'll not go," repeated the old woman. "We'll not be parted. Leave us be. *Please.*"

"All right," said Jessica, puzzled, "but we don't mean you any harm."

James said, "I'll just refill your pail as it was my fault you dropped it."

They watched him, still suspicious, as he went to the stream and then came back with a full pail.

"Thank 'ee," said the old woman. "That was kind."

"If you bain't looking for us, what are you doing here?" asked the old man curiously.

"Just exploring," James answered.

"We found the ruined cottages and saw the smoke from your chimney."

"I told 'ee, Martha, that would give us away one day," said the old man.

"But we have to cook," she insisted, "and nobody's ever come nigh here until now."

"Because I scare 'em off." To the twins' surprise, the old man chuckled.

Then Jessica knew what he meant. "*You're* the ghost. You make the moaning sounds that scare people."

"That be right, missy," he said, smiling at her. "Only don't 'ee tell anyone."

"I won't. I promise," said Jessica. "But why are you so frightened of being found?"

"*I know!*" James exclaimed. "You're trespassing on Squire Basset's land."

The old man shook his head. "This bain't Squire's land. It belongs to Lord

Berridge. He spends most of his time in London — gambling, so 'tis said — so his gamekeeper takes it easy and never comes this way."

The old couple looked at one another. Then the woman said, "We'd best tell them, Simon." She turned to the twins. "But will you promise to keep our secret?"

"Oh, yes!" they answered promptly, for they could not believe that this harmless-looking old couple needed to hide because they had done something wicked.

Martha sat down stiffly on the broken wall. "'Tis the Poor Law authorities we're afraid of. They'd send us to the workhouse."

"But that's for paupers!" James exclaimed.

The old people looked so hurt that Jessica said quickly, "Papa says lots of people can't help being poor if they're not paid enough."

"Oh, we were paid enough to live on when we were working," said Simon bitterly, "but as soon as we got beyond it . . . I was carpenter on Squire Basset's estate and my wife helped in the laundry. But we're both over seventy now and my hands are rheumaticky and Martha's back won't stand up to the heavy work. We could have looked after ourselves with a bit of help from parish relief if only we'd been allowed to stay in our cottage. But Squire wanted it for the new carpenter so we had to leave. And that meant the workhouse, and being parted after fifty years together."

"Why should you be parted?" asked Jessica.

"'Tis one of the rules."

"But that's cruel!"

"Haven't you any family who'd help you?" James asked.

"We raised three sons but they saw no future here and went off to Canada."

"How do you manage?" asked Jessica, glancing towards the tumble-down cottage.

"Well enough, in this weather," answered Martha. "Simon snares rabbits and catches fish and pigeons sometimes, and we go out of a night and help ourselves to a turnip or a few potatoes."

"Hush, Martha," her husband warned.

"We won't tell," James assured them. "But isn't it dangerous, with traps and . . . ?"

"There bain't any traps in these woods and I never venture on Squire's land."

Jessica asked, "May we see inside your cottage?"

"If you like," said Martha, rising with a hand to her back. "'Tis no palace, as you can imagine."

There was only one room, with bracken strewn over the earth floor and sacking fastened over the two windows which had lost their glass. A pile of heather covered by a single blanket formed their bed and the only furniture was a rickety table and a couple of three-legged stools. Beside the hearth was a cooking-pot and some plates and knives and forks, and little else.

Jessica, thinking of the comfort of their own home, was shocked, but James said, "I'd like to live like this."

Simon smiled. "In summer, mebbe, but come winter . . . "

"Even then," said Martha stoutly, "'twill be better than the workhouse, living with strangers, and all those rules. And bearing the shame of it. That would be almost the worst part. For we had a nice little home before we were forced out of it."

"And we could only bring a few things with us," Simon added, "leaving by night as we did, so's folks could tell Squire truthfully they didn't know what'd happened to us."

"We'll help," said Jessica impulsively. "I don't know how, yet, but we will, won't we, James?"

"Yes," said James promptly, and put

a hand in his pocket. "Do you like raisins?"

"Raisins?" repeated Martha in surprise. "They're a rare treat in our lives, I can tell you."

James tipped a handful on to a plate. "I'm afraid they're a bit grubby from my pocket but they'll taste just as good."

Martha hugged them both. "What kind children you be, and we don't even know your names."

"James and Jessica Milner," said Jessica, "and our father is the new doctor and we live at Foxton House. And we'd better be getting back now or we'll be late for lunch."

"I'll show 'ee an easier way, through the wood," Simon offered.

He led them across the clearing to a narrow track winding upwards through the trees.

"That'll take 'ee to the lane," he told them, and stood waving until they were out of sight.

The twins were unusually silent on their way home, both trying to think up a plan to help their new friends without breaking their promise of secrecy.

When they reached home, Molly exclaimed, "What a pickle you two are in! You'd better clean yourselves up before lunch. I could spend a day black-berrying and not get in half such a state! And where *are* the blackberries, may I ask?"

The twins looked at one another in dismay. Then James said, "We hid them while we went for a walk, and then forgot them. We'll fetch them tomorrow."

And that, thought James, would provide a good reason for their returning to Badgers' Wood in the morning.

Chapter 2

AT LUNCH MRS Milner looked happier than at any time since moving to Devonshire.

"The parson's wife called on me this morning," she told her family. "She asked me to organise some sewing parties to provide clothes for the poor of the parish, which will also be an excellent opportunity for me to meet some other ladies, although I do not suppose it will be such genteel company as I was used to in Bath."

"The help is much needed," said Dr Milner. "Perhaps you could invite

the Squire's lady. Then you could suggest that if her husband was less harsh on his tenants, there would not be so many distressing cases *needing* help."

"I would not think she has any influence on her husband at all," Mrs Milner retorted. "She is a little mouse of a creature, completely dominated by that dreadful man. I shall send Molly up to the loft this afternoon to look through the trunks we stored there when we moved. I'm not sure what is in them but there must be *some* outgrown or outmoded clothes suitable for alteration."

"Jessica and I could do that," James said eagerly.

His sister followed his lead. "We'd know better than Molly what you'd want to keep, Mama."

"What a splendid idea!" said their father. "You can play at dressing-up and be useful at the same time."

Up in the loft, the twins started rummaging eagerly in trunks and boxes.

"What a bit of luck!" James exclaimed. "There must be lots of things here which will be useful for Simon and Martha. These trousers for a start."

"And here's one of Grandmama's dresses. Mama would never wear purple but Martha would be glad of it,

I'm sure. And a warm shawl, a bit frayed but that won't matter."

"Here are some candles, they'll be useful. And — oh, look!" James laughed as he held up a child's hat covered with rosebuds and violets and little bows. "You could wear that to church," he suggested, ramming it on his sister's head.

She looked at herself in an old mirror tucked between the folds of a white blanket.

"Most becoming," she said, copying her mother's voice, then giggled. "I can't see Martha in *that*."

James was suddenly serious. "I suppose it's all right, taking these things without Mama knowing."

"Of course it is," said Jessica, returning to her rummaging. "We're helping the poor, like Mama, only we have to keep quiet about it because of our promise."

"How are we to get all this to the cottage?"

"We could take some in my dolls' pram."

"We can't get a pram down through Badgers' Wood."

"We can hide it amongst the trees and carry the stuff down."

"Yes, all right," agreed James a little reluctantly because he had not thought of it first. Then he brightened. "I could pretend to be going fishing and take some things in my bag."

"That's a good idea. We'll have to get them downstairs when nobody's about, though, and not take too much at once."

"Let's tell Mama there's more here than we can sort out in one afternoon."

"And that would be true," said Jessica, triumphantly holding up a pair of Hessian boots. "These are so old-fashioned I don't think Papa would ever wear them again but they'll keep Simon's feet dry when it rains."

The weather stayed fine so that Jessica taking her dolls for an outing every day, accompanied by James carrying his fishing tackle seemed a perfectly natural sight. Their mother, busy with preparations for her first sewing party, was glad to have them out of the house and Cook, fully occupied with preparing the refreshments Mrs Milner thought necessary for such an occasion, did not notice when some bread and dripping and sugar disappeared from the larder.

Simon and Martha were as happy and excited as children being given a special birthday treat each day.

"Soon this tumbledown cottage will *be* a palace," said Martha, spreading two slightly moth-eaten blankets over their makeshift bed, then making an effort to straighten her back to show off the purple dress.

Simon stuffed his old boots in a crack in the wall. "If I leave them there, mebbe a robin'll nest in one come next spring."

With James' help he made a better job of the roof, adding bracken to the old thatch. He taught James how to use the tools his own fingers were now too stiff to manage and so the table was repaired.

Glass, salvaged from one of the other cottages, replaced the sacking in the two windows.

Jessica went foraging with Martha, collecting firewood, gathering blackberries and mushrooms and crab-apples and Martha taught her the names of many birds and flowers. They rested by the stream in Jessica's favourite place and Martha recounted tales of her childhood and they played noughts and crosses with sticks and stones.

"It's more fun here than in Bath," declared the twins.

"You've certainly brought some fun back into our lives," said Simon.

And Martha added, "'Tis like having our grandchildren here, the ones in Canada we'll never see."

Chapter 3

ON THE MORNING of their mother's sewing party, the twins were in the kitchen when Molly came hurrying in.

"Such news I've just heard in the village," she burst out. "Lord Berridge has got so badly in debt, gambling, he's had to sell off part of his estate. And who d'you think has bought it?"

"Not Squire Basset?" said Cook, and when Molly nodded, she raised her floury hands in dismay. "That's bad news, indeed!"

"You're right. He'll be raising rents and no doubt putting up PRIVATE notices to keep the village children from the bluebell woods. They say his gamekeeper is already at work putting down traps and chasing any vagrants off the land."

"What are vagrants?" asked Jessica.

"Folks without any real homes."

The twins looked at one another in alarm.

"What will happen to these people?" James asked.

"They'll be told to clear off, move to another parish, or sent to the workhouse."

Jessica tugged at James' sleeve. "We must warn Simon and Martha," she whispered.

"I know. But we can't go yet, we have to meet Mama's sewing ladies."

"What are you two whispering about?" demanded Cook suspiciously. "And what are you hiding in your pockets?"

Reluctantly they brought out some cakes and biscuits.

"Shame on you! Anyone would think you weren't given enough to eat."

"They're not for *us*," Jessica blurted out, and winced as James pinched her arm.

Cook, raking the stove, had not heard but Molly gave the twins a thoughtful look and when Jessica left the kitchen Molly followed her to her bedroom.

"You two are up to something, I reckon," she said. "I've young brothers and sisters and I know the signs. For one thing, your dolls seem to be sitting very high in their pram. And I found two extra blankets under Master James' mattress that aren't there now. So what mischief are you up to?"

"It's not mischief, Molly, truly. But it *is* a secret. Please don't tell on us."

"All right, but don't take any more food or Cook may report it to the mistress and then you'll be in trouble."

Dressed in their Sunday clothes, the twins were presented to the ladies of the sewing party. Politely they answered the grown-ups' tiresome questions and tried not to show their impatience to be off to the secret valley. When at last they were released they raced upstairs to change their clothes, then slipped out of the garden gate. They were running along the lane when they were confronted by Squire Basset, riding his big, grey horse. He reined in, blocking their path.

"Where are you two going in such a hurry?" he shouted.

"We . . ." As Jessica hesitated, James said, "We were having a race."

"Hmph! When *I* was a boy I raced with other boys, not *my sister*. Girls can't run properly."

As Jessica was about to protest, a pigeon clattered from a tree, startling

the horse. While the Squire was bringing it under control the twins slipped past and ran on towards Badgers' Wood. Just before they reached it, James climbed up a high bank to make sure the Squire could not see them turn down the track to the valley.

"It's all right. He's riding along the

top of the field where we picked blackberries."

"I suppose *that* belongs to him now and there'll soon be a notice up. Do you think he might ride into the valley?"

"No," said James, jumping down, "it's too steep for his horse."

"Then I wish he *would*, and break his neck!" Jessica declared fiercely. "Squire Basset, I mean, not the poor horse."

When they gave the news about Squire Basset to Simon and Martha, the old couple looked so distressed that Jessica's anger turned to tears. She put an arm around Martha as they sat on a broken wall.

"We thought we were safe here," the old woman said pathetically, "but we can't stay if 'tis Squire Basset's land."

"You'm right," agreed Simon wearily. "We'll have to move on."

"Where can you go?" asked James. "If only you'd let us tell our parents, I'm sure they'd help."

Simon shook his head. "They'd more likely say we should take the places offered in the workhouse and are lucky to have the chance of a roof over our heads."

"*Lucky*!" exclaimed Jessica. "To be driven from your home just because you're old. It's so unfair and cruel!"

Her voice had risen and James warned, "Not so loud, Jess. If anyone's around, you'll give us away." He turned to Simon. "Do you think you ought to put out the fire? The smoke was how we found you in the first place."

"You'm right, lad," said Simon.

"We'd best leave tonight," said Martha, "when 'tis dark."

"There must be *something* we can do," said Jessica desperately. "We can't just let you . . ." She broke off as James raised a warning hand.

"Listen," he whispered. "I think someone is up in the wood."

Suddenly there was a crashing in the undergrowth and a man's voice, grumbling and swearing.

"Squire's gamekeeper!" whispered Martha in dismay. "We must leave now, at once."

"No, wait," said James. "I've an idea."

Telling them all to hide in the cottage, he fetched a white blanket, dodged across the clearing and disappeared amongst the buildings of the

deserted village. As the old couple and Jessica huddled together, from the direction of the derelict cottages came a weird, unearthly wailing. Martha's eyes grew wide with fear and even Jessica felt an icy shiver up and down her spine. Then came the startled voice of

the gamekeeper. "Oh, God save me!" he cried, and then in sheer terror, "No! No! Keep away. Don't come near me!"

"It must be James," whispered Jessica, and peered cautiously out of the door.

The gamekeeper was standing amongst the trees above the ruined village, holding a gun and some traps. He was staring with horrified eyes at a shapeless white form advancing towards him. Again came the spine-chilling wails. The white form swayed from side to side and raised trailing folds like ghostly arms, threatening the gamekeeper. For a few moments it seemed as if the gamekeeper could not move. Then, dropping the traps, he turned and fled up through the trees.

Jessica ran across the clearing and hugged her brother.

"James, you were wonderful! Really scary!"

James threw off the blanket. "*I* was a bit scared, too, when I saw his gun. But it was fun!"

Simon and Martha were laughing in their relief. Then Simon said, "You did well, lad, but 'twouldn't have worked had it been Squire himself. *He'd* not believe in ghosties."

"Squire Basset never goes anywhere without his horse," said James, "and he can't ride it down here. He's more likely to see you if you leave the valley."

"The lad's right, Martha," said Simon. "Mebbe 'tis best to bide a while longer."

As the twins left the wood they heard voices from further along the lane.

"Squire Basset," said Jessica, "and he sounds angry."

James climbed the bank again. "He's having a row with his gamekeeper. Listen!"

The gamekeeper was protesting

loudly. "'*Twas* a ghost, I tell 'ee, sir, coming at me, moaning and screeching like the devil himself."

"Don't be such a damned fool!" roared the Squire. "I'll wager it was a poacher and he'll be down there now, with a brace of pheasants in his bag, laughing his head off. Get after him at once."

"I'll not!" the man declared, his voice rising. "Everyone knows that place be haunted. I'll not go down there again."

"Then I'll go, myself, damn you! Open that gate."

"It's the gate into the field beside Badgers' Wood," James told Jessica.

The gamekeeper protested again, his voice high-pitched with anxiety. "You can't ride down there, sir, 'tis . . . "

"Open that gate, or you'll feel my whip across your shoulders."

"I *must* see what's happening," said Jessica, and scrambled up beside her brother.

They saw the gate swing inwards, the grey horse plunge forward. The game-keeper came running along the lane so fast he did not even see the twins. He was talking to himself, sounding very frightened.

"If he breaks his neck, 'twon't be my fault. But I'll not be witness to it."

The Squire had cantered across the field and was putting his horse to the steep, uneven ground leading down to the stream. It started down gingerly, urged on by whip and spur.

"Poor horse," said Jessica. "I hope . . . "

Her words were cut short by the frightened whinny of the horse as it fell. The Squire was thrown over its head and landed with a great thud amongst the bracken. The horse regained its feet and bolted. Squire Basset lay where he had fallen.

The twins looked anxiously at one another.

"Do you think he *has* broken his neck?" asked Jessica in an awed whisper.

James, trying to sound braver than he felt, said, "I think we'd better go and see. He might be hurt and needing help."

"Why should we help *him*? He's horrid and cruel and . . . "

"Papa says anyone ill or hurt must be helped," James said firmly.

They climbed down and ran along the lane, in through the open gateway and across the field.

The Squire lay on his back, his eyes

closed. His right leg was at an odd angle. James knelt beside him and felt for a pulse, as he had seen his father do.

"He's still alive. We'd better fetch Papa."

"We don't know where to find him."

"He might be at home. He promised to come back in time to meet the sewing ladies. Run and see, Jess."

"Aren't you coming?"

James shook his head and tried to look very grown-up. "I'll stay in case he regains consciousness. Then I can tell him help is on the way. If you meet anyone . . . "

"I'll tell them what's happened and ask them to come. I'll be as quick as I can."

Jessica ran all the way home without seeing anyone, but to her relief her father's gig was in the drive. She ran full tilt into the house and burst into the drawing-room, so out of breath that, confronted by a circle of astonished faces and her mother, demanding, "Jessica, how dare you!", she could not answer.

Her father came quickly across the room and put an arm round her. "What is it, Jess? Has something happened to James?"

She shook her head. "No. It . . . it's the Squire," she gasped.

The ladies leaned forward, their eyes bright with curiosity. Mrs Milner made to rise but her husband said quietly, "Leave this to me, my dear."

He picked Jessica up and carried her into the hall, shutting the door behind him.

"Get your breath back, then tell me."

When she had blurted it all out, he said, "I'll go at once. Will you come with me, to show me the field?"

"Oh, yes!" she said eagerly, and then she was up in the gig beside her father, who would take charge and know exactly what to do.

Chapter 4

IT RAINED HEAVILY during the night and the weather next morning was still damp and drizzly but that did not prevent a number of the sewing ladies calling at Foxton House. They *said* they had come to ask Mrs Milner's advice about clothes they were altering but it was obvious their real reason was to find out all they could about Squire Basset's accident.

"He regained consciousness just before my husband arrived," the twins' mother told them. "His right leg was broken and he was carried home on a hurdle by four men from Deerleap Farm. My husband went ahead to warn Mrs Basset but as soon as the Squire was within sight of the manor, he began shouting for his groom, ordering him to catch his horse and give it a sound whipping. Fortunately, the horse has not yet been found, and neither has that heavy whip the Squire always carries . . . "

"I think we must all agree," said the parson's wife, "that but for your brave and sensible children he might well have died, alone in that field. I do hope that when he is sufficiently recovered he will realise that and show his appreciation."

"Some hope!" said James, when he and Jessica were at last freed from being petted and praised. "Can you imagine the Squire giving us a reward for saving his life?"

"If he did, I wouldn't take it," Jessica declared fiercely. "I *wanted* him to break his neck and I'm sorry he didn't. And I don't care if it's wicked to say so. Oh, I do hope Simon and Martha didn't get wet in last night's storm."

"Let's go and see," James suggested, "and we can give them some good news. With the Squire out of action and his gamekeeper scared off, they ought to be safe for a bit longer."

"Oh, yes!" agreed Jessica eagerly. "Let's go at once."

They ran along the lane, dodging puddles, but at the wood they had to slow down for the rain had made the track very slippery. James lost his footing and slid down the last part on his back, getting plastered with mud.

"You'll catch it if Mama sees you," said Jessica, and then, she too, slithered down the last few yards and landed on her knees.

They were laughing together when James noticed there was no smoke coming from the chimney.

"I suppose they were too frightened to light a fire," he said.

"But they must have been so cold, and perhaps wet, after last night's storm."

They called softly as they approached the cottage but neither Simon nor Martha came out to greet them as usual. When they knocked there was no answer, nor any sound from inside.

"Perhaps they've gone to fetch water," Jessica suggested.

But when they went down to the stream, there was nobody there.

"Perhaps they're ill," said Jessica, anxiously. "I think we ought to look."

They knocked again, then quietly opened the door.

The cottage was empty. All the things the twins had brought had gone.

Only a battered pot, the ashes in the hearth and the bed of heather showed that anyone had been living there.

"They've left!" exclaimed Jessica in dismay. "Oh, why . . . ?"

"They must have been so frightened by what happened yesterday. But they would have waited for the rain to stop, surely, so they can't have gone far. Come on, let's look for them."

"But we don't know which way . . . "

"There'll be footprints in the mud," said James confidently. "Let's spread out."

But although they quartered the ground around the cottage and searched among the ruined buildings and at the foot of the wood, the only prints were those of deer and fox and badger.

"They must have left yesterday," said James, "and the rain has washed away all trace."

"Then what can we do?"

"Try and think which way they'd have gone."

"It would have been away from the village, wouldn't it? And if they went at night, and carrying all those belongings, they might have risked the lane."

"Yes," James agreed. "It's worth trying. Come on."

They scrambled up the track through the wood, slipping and slithering, not caring how plastered they became with the sticky mud. They had just reached the lane when James stopped and pointed.

"Look! On that holly bush. Surely that's wool from the shawl you gave Martha."

Jessica ran to have a closer look. "Yes, you're right. So they did go along the lane. Oh, James, we *must* find them! It's just not fair if we saved Squire Basset's life but can't help Simon and Martha."

"We'll find them," said James, with more confidence than he felt. "We must look for other clues. You take that side of the lane and I'll stay on this. Search the ground as well as in the hedge. They may have dropped things."

James was right. Soon Jessica found a fork in the long grass of the verge and a little further on James stumbled on Simon's hammer. Then for a while they

found nothing but there were no side turnings the couple could have turned down so the twins plodded on, methodically searching. They came to a field full of sheep, with a shepherd's hut in one corner. James was bending down, to examine the ground near the gateway, when Jessica exclaimed, "*There they are*, running from the hut! And — oh, James, there's a man chasing them!"

"*The gamekeeper*! And he's got the Squire's riding-whip. Come on, Jess, quick!"

He tried to open the gate but the fastening was rusty so he clambered up and jumped down the other side. But for Jessica, with her full skirts, it was not so easy. Impatiently he stopped to help her, then they were racing across the field, scattering the sheep.

Simon and Martha had stopped running and were facing the gamekeeper, pleading with him. Martha was half-bent, a hand to her back.

"You know us, Ned, we're not doing any harm."

"Aren't you, indeed? Squire arranged for you to be found places in the workhouse. So what are you doing here, trespassing on his land? You just wait until he hears about this!"

"He *won't* hear about it!"

James' clear voice startled the gamekeeper. As the man turned to face him, James said, "You won't tell Squire Basset because if you do *we* shall tell him, and everybody else in the district, that you were frightened of a ghost. This ghost!" James started moaning and wailing just as he had by the deserted village. "Only I had a white blanket covering me yesterday."

The gamekeeper looked at first incredulous, then very angry. He lunged towards James, the heavy whip raised. Simon rushed forward but was pushed roughly to the ground. James lowered his head and butted the gamekeeper in the stomach. As the man doubled up,

gasping, Jessica snatched the whip.

"Don't you *dare* hit my brother!" she yelled. "And don't you *dare* hurt Simon and Martha. They're our friends and we *won't* let them be taken to the workhouse."

"You little spitfire!" the gamekeeper shouted and made a grab for the whip. Then he stopped, his hand still outstretched, and turned his head towards the lane, listening.

They all heard the clip-clop of hooves, and then into view above the hedge came the head and shoulders of Dr Milner, driving his gig along the lane.

At the tops of their voices, the twins called to him.

"Papa! Papa! Help us!"

Their father reined in, vaulted from his gig over the gate, and ran towards them. The gamekeeper ran, too, in the opposite direction.

Jessica threw her arms around her father. "Oh, Papa, you came just in time. That horrid man was going to take Simon and Martha away and we were trying to save them but it's Squire Basset's land and . . . "

"Take it easy, Jess," her father said, "and tell me just what you two have been up to."

James glanced at Simon and Martha, who were clinging together, looking nearly as frightened as when the twins had first seen them.

"I don't think we can keep our promise any longer. I think we have to tell our father now."

The old couple nodded hopelessly. "You'm right, lad," said Simon. "Despite all you two have done for us, we're beaten. 'Tis the workhouse for us now, sure enough."

Jessica ran to them. "No, no. Papa won't allow it. It will be all right, you'll see."

Dr Milner looked at each one in turn, a thoughtful, considering look. Then he said, "Well, children, suppose you start at the beginning."

Chapter 5

"IT IS DISGRACEFUL that these old people should have been treated in this way," declared Mrs Milner when she was told the whole story. "If only you had told us before."

"But we couldn't, Mama," James pointed out. "We'd given our promise."

"Yes, of course, I had forgotten. Now, I will make you one. Your old couple will not be sent to the workhouse. Instead, they will be back in their own cottage within a week."

"Mama!" the twins exclaimed in astonishment, and their father asked,

"How do you propose to work this miracle, my dear?"

"I shall visit Mr Basset," Mrs Milner replied determinedly, "and point out to him that but for our children he might not now be alive. This very morning the parson's wife was saying just that and it was generally agreed that he should be expected to show them some appreciation." She turned to the twins. "Can you think of a better reward for saving his life?"

"No, Mama!" they said in unison. "That would be wonderful. When will you go?"

"This afternoon, if your father thinks Mr Basset is well enough to receive me. You may come with me if you wish, just for the drive."

With the twins beside her, looking very different from the bedraggled figures their father had brought home after they had all helped Simon and Martha back to the cottage in the valley, Mrs Milner set out for the Manor, driving her husband's gig.

"It would have been preferable, naturally," she remarked, "had we arrived in my father's carriage, with a footman in attendance, but I have no doubt I shall manage very well."

The twins were delighted. Their mother was again as she had been in Bath, elegant, self-assured and looking

quite happy and as they watched her enter the manor house they wished they could see the Squire's face for not even a duchess, they thought, could have appeared more impressive.

Impatiently they waited outside, with James at the pony's head and Jessica perched on the high seat of the gig, passing the time by naming all the birds in sight, which Martha had taught her to do.

At last their mother reappeared. Beside her was a small, drab-looking woman whom she introduced to the twins as the Squire's wife. As they were about to leave, Mrs Basset said, "It was so kind of you to call and enquire after my husband's health, Mrs Milner, and I am so pleased to have met your two dear children who, even *he* has to admit, saved his life."

Their mother said, smiling, "And it was kind of *you*, Mrs Basset, to spare the time to write the document for your husband to sign. It will please James and Jessica so much."

"What will please us, Mama?" demanded Jessica, as soon as they were out of earshot. "What document has Squire Basset signed?"

Their mother reined in just beyond the manor gates and produced a folded piece of paper from her purse.

"This one," she said triumphantly. "Mr Basset has agreed to find another cottage for the new estate carpenter so that your friends Simon and Martha may return to their old home. This document guarantees that they can remain there, rent free, for the rest of their lives."

"Oh, Mama! That's wonderful!"